KU-348-733

CARNIVAL CLASSICS

JUST SO STORIES

Abridged by Charles Moritz
from the story by Rudyard Kipling
Illustrated by Charles Fuge

Carnival

An Imprint of HarperCollins *Publishers*

HOW THE ELEPHANT GOT ITS TRUNK

The elephant has not always had a trunk, long ago he only had a blackish, bulging nose about the size of a boot. And that is how things stayed until one day, along came a baby elephant who lived in Africa and who was always asking questions about everything and everyone under the sun.

He asked his tall aunt, the ostrich, why her tail feathers grew the way they did. She thought he was very rude and spanked him with her bony claw. He asked his uncle, the giraffe, what made his skin so spotty. His uncle thought the baby elephant was very cheeky and spanked him with his hard hoof.

But still the baby elephant kept on with his questions. He asked his broad aunt, the hippopotamus, why her eyes were red. She was so put out she spanked him as well with her broad hoof. Then he asked his hairy uncle, the baboon, why melons tasted the way they did. Uncle baboon thought it was such a silly question that he spanked him too with his hairy paw.

Still the baby elephant kept on asking more and more questions. And though his uncles and aunts grew so impatient with him that they kept on spanking him – still he could not stop.

One day this baby elephant thought up a fine new question that he'd never asked before. "What does the crocodile have for dinner?" Straightaway everybody said to him, "Hush!". Then they all spanked him without stopping for a long time.

Later the baby elephant met the Kolokolo bird sitting in the middle of a thorn bush and told him, "Everyone has spanked me. My father, my mother and all my aunts and uncles too. Just because I can't stop asking questions. But the thing I really want to know is what does the crocodile have for his dinner. Can you tell me?"

The Kolokolo bird gave a sad cry then told him, "Go to the banks of the great grey-green greasy Limpopo River, where the banks are lined with fever trees and there you will find out."

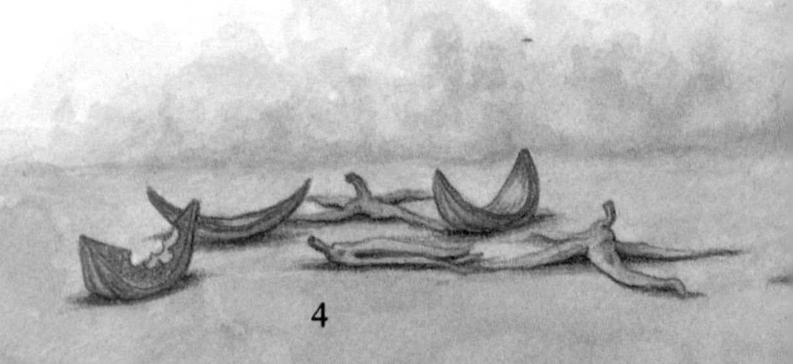

The very next morning the baby elephant took a hundred pounds of bananas, a hundred pounds of sugar cane and seventeen melons and said goodbye to all his family, telling them, "I am going to the great grey-green greasy Limpopo River where the banks are lined with fever trees so I can find out what the crocodile has for his dinner." And do you know what they did? They all spanked him once more for luck.

So, feeling rather uncomfortable, he set off, eating melons and leaving a trail of skins on the ground because he could not pick them up. He travelled for many miles, chewing at melons all the while, until he reached the banks of the great grey-green greasy Limpopo River which was lined with fever trees, just as the Kolokolo bird had said.

But the baby elephant had a problem. He had never seen a crocodile, so he had no idea what one looked like. The first animal he came across was a stripy python, curled around a rock.

"Excuse me," said the baby elephant politely, "but have you seen such a thing as a crocodile anywhere around here?"

"Have I seen a crocodile?" said the stripy python. "Why whatever next? Of course I've seen a crocodile!"

"Well then, could you kindly tell me what he has for his dinner," asked the baby elephant.

The stripy python quickly uncoiled himself from around the rock and spanked the baby elephant with his scaly tail.

"I just don't understand it," said the poor confused baby elephant. "Everyone keeps spanking me when I ask what the crocodile has for dinner. And now you've spanked me too."

So he said goodbye to the python, and helped to coil him round the rock again. Then he went on his way munching melons. All at once he trod on what he thought was a log at the very edge of the great grey-green greasy Limpopo River. But actually that log was a crocodile. The crocodile winked one eye at him.

"Excuse me," said the baby elephant most politely, "but have you seen a crocodile anywhere around here?" The crocodile winked his other eye and lifted half his tail out of the mud. Seeing this, the baby elephant stepped back politely because he did not want to be spanked again.

"Don't by shy little one," said the crocodile, "come over here. I am the crocodile. You've found me."

The baby elephant was very excited, "You're the very person I've been trying to find for days and days now. Please tell me...what do you have for your dinner?"

"Come closer, little one," said the crocodile, "and I'll whisper it to you."

So the baby elephant put his head down close to the crocodile's big toothy mouth, and in a flash, the crocodile caught him sharply by his little nose. "Today," said the crocodile through his clenched teeth, "I think I'll begin with baby elephant."

Well, the baby elephant was very annoyed at being tricked. "Led go! You are hurting be!" he shouted through his squashed nose.

Luckily, just then the stripy python slithered down the river bank. "My young friend. Save yourself. Pull as hard as you can or that crocodile will pull you into the water before you can say 'Jack Robinson'."

So, the baby elephant leaned back on his hind legs and pulled and pulled. He pulled so hard his nose began to stretch. The crocodile slid back into the water and he too pulled with all his strength.

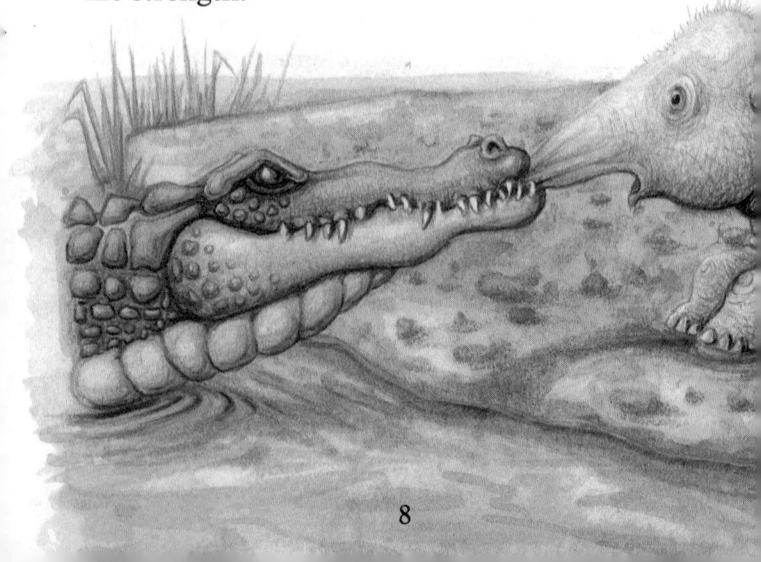

To try and get free, the baby elephant spread his four legs wide and pulled all the more. Still his nose kept on stretching. Then the crocodile started to paddle with his tail to help him pull even harder. And all the while the baby elephant's nose grew longer and longer. Suddenly the baby elephant felt his legs slipping. By now his nose was nearly five feet long, and as he slipped towards the river he wailed through it, "This is too butch for be!"

Seeing the fix he was in, the stripy python came to the rescue. Knotting himself around the baby elephant's back legs he started to pull and together they pulled the hardest. At last the crocodile let go of the baby elephant's nose and let it fall into the river with a loud plop.

Quite exhausted, the baby elephant slumped down on the bank, thanking the python. Next he took care of his poor pulled nose by wrapping it up in cool banana leaves, and dipping it in the great grey-green greasy Limpopo to cool.

"Why on earth are you doing that?" asked the python.

"Excuse me," said the baby elephant, "but now my nose is badly out of shape so I'm waiting for the water to make it shrink again."

"Then you'll have to wait a very long time," said the python. "Besides, it seems to me, some people don't know when they're well off."

Well the baby elephant sat there for three whole days but his nose never grew any shorter. He watched it for so long his eyes went into a squint. What had happened, you see, was that the crocodile had pulled it right out into a trunk just the same as the ones you see on every elephant today. At the end of the third day, a fly came along and bit him on the shoulder. Before the baby elephant even thought about what he was doing, he lifted up his trunk and, with one quick swish, he knocked the fly dead.

"Aha!" said the python. "You couldn't have done that with your little old nose, could you? Why don't you have something to eat now?"

Again, without even thinking what he was doing, the baby elephant stretched out his trunk, plucked a large bundle of grass, dusted it clean against his front legs, and then stuffed it in his mouth.

"There you are!" cried the python. "There's another trick you couldn't have done with your little old nose. Don't you think the sun is very hot here?"

"Yes it is," agreed the baby elephant, and before he thought what he was doing, he scooped up a schloop of mud from the banks of the great grey-green greasy Limpopo with his trunk, and slapped it on his head, where it made a cool, schloopy sloshy mud cap which trickled down behind the ears.

"Well, just look at that," said the python. "You couldn't have done that with your little old nose, could you? Now then how do you feel about being spanked again?"

"Excuse me," said the baby elephant, "but I wouldn't like it at all,"

"Well then, how would you like to spank somebody else? "asked the python.

"Oh yes, I'd like that very much indeed," answered the baby elephant.

"Well I think you'll find that new nose of yours will come in very handy," said the python.

"Thank you," said the baby elephant. "I'll remember that. Now if you don't mind I think I'll go home to my dear family and try my new nose out."

And so the baby elephant made his way home right across Africa. Whenever he wanted fruit, he pulled it down from a tree, instead of waiting for it to fall as he used to. If he wanted grass to eat, he no longer had to kneel down to get it. Instead he'd pull it out of the ground. When the flies bit him, he'd break off the branch of a tree and use it as a fly whisk. And whenever the sun grew too hot, he'd make himself a new, cooling, slushy-squashy mud cap to wear. Whenever he felt lonely he sang to himself down his trunk with a noise louder than several brass bands. He specially went out of his way to find a broad hippopotamus and spanked him very hard indeed, just to make sure the python had told him the truth about his new trunk. And the rest of the time, he used his trunk to pick up the melon skins he'd dropped on his way to the Limpopo.

At last, one dark evening, he reached home and found all his dear family. He coiled up his trunk and bellowed, "How do you do?"

They were very glad to see him and straightaway said, "Come here and let us spank you for wandering off asking so many questions."

"Oh no," said the baby elephant. "I don't think you people really know anything about spanking. But I do. Let me show you,"

Then he uncurled his trunk and knocked two of his dear brothers head over heels.

"Oh bananas!" they said. "Where did you learn to do that, and what has happened to your nose?"

"I got a new one from the crocodile on the banks of the great grey-green greasy Limpopo River," the baby elephant told them. And with that he picked up his hairy uncle by one hairy leg and tossed him into a hornets' nest. Then, to their great surprise, that bad baby elephant spanked all his dear family for a long time, until they all had very warm bottoms indeed.

His dear family got so fed up that one by one they all hurried off to the great grey-green Limpopo River to borrow new noses from the crocodile too. When they came back, nobody spanked anybody any more.

Ever since that day, every elephant you'll ever see has a trunk exactly like the one the crocodile gave to the nosey little baby elephant by the river that day.

HOW THE RHINOCEROS GOT HIS SKIN

Once upon a time on a lonely island by the shores of the Red Sea, there lived a Parsee man. He wore a fine hat which shone in the rays of the sun and he lived there all alone with just his knife and a small cooking stove for company.

One day he took flour and water, some currants, plums and sugar and made himself a big cake. It was two feet across and three feet thick, and he baked it till it turned a rich brown colour and smelled most delicious.

Then the Parsee sat down to eat it. But just at that moment, out of the wild forest walked a huge rhinoceros with two piggy eyes and a fierce looking horn on his nose. The sun shone brightly off the rhino's smooth skin, for in those days it fitted him tightly with not a wrinkle to be seen.

Now this rhino was a bad-mannered beast. He was then and he still is today. Seeing the Parsee he gave a loud rough grunt. Quick as a flash the Parsee left his cake and climbed to the top of a palm tree for safety.

Then the rhinoceros pushed the oil stove over with his nose so that the cake rolled along the ground. He spiked it on the horn of his nose and, waving his tail, he lumbered off back into the wild forest. When he had gone, the Parsee came down from the palm tree and put his stove back up on its legs. He was very annoyed that the greedy rhino had taken his cake.

Five weeks later it was so hot everybody took off all their clothes. Even the Parsee man took off his hat. And the rhinoceros undid three buttons underneath his body and took off his smooth, tight-fitting skin. He carried it over his shoulder and came down to the water to bathe. Leaving his skin on the beach, he walked straight into the water and blew bubbles through his nose.

Soon after, the Parsee came by and found the rhino's skin. He smiled a huge smile and then he scurried back to his camp and filled his fine hat full of cake crumbs. Now, the Parsee never ate anything else but cake and he never swept out his camp. So he had a fine store of crumbs. He took the rhino's skin and shook it and scrubbed it and rubbed it full of as many old, dry, tickly cake crumbs as it would hold. Then he replaced the rhino's skin on the beach, climbed to the top of his palm tree and waited.

Very soon the rhino came dripping out of the water and put his skin back on. It tickled like mad - just like cake crumbs in bed. It made him want to scratch, but that only made things worse. So then he tried lying down on the sand and rolling over and over. But every time he rolled, the cake crumbs tickled him even more.

Finally, quite desperate, he ran to the palm tree and rubbed himself against it. He rubbed so much and so hard that he rubbed his skin into a great fold over his shoulders. Then another fold appeared where the rhino had rubbed his buttons off. And as he kept rubbing, trying to stop the terrible itching, more folds appeared on his legs.

Finally the rhino went home very angry indeed and horribly scratchy. And from that day to this, every rhinoceros has great folds in its skin and a terrible temper too. All because of those cake crumbs itching away inside.

THE CRAB THAT PLAYED WITH THE SEA

A very long time ago, before any animals lived on the earth, the Eldest Magician was very busy indeed. First he had to get the earth ready and when he'd done all that, then he had to get the sea ready. Only then did he tell all the animals that they could come out and play.

The animals said, "O Eldest Magician, what shall we play at?"

"I will show you," said the Eldest Magician. Then he took all the elephants and said, "Play at being elephants." Next he took all the beavers and said, "Play at being beavers." He did the same with all the cows and turtles and carried on until he had taken nearly all the birds, beasts and fish on the earth and in the sea, and had told them to play at being themselves. Towards evening the Eldest Magician spotted Man coming towards him with his little daughter sitting on his shoulders.

"What is all this play I see?" Man asked him. The Eldest Magician stopped his work and said, "Ho, Son of Adam, this is the play of the Very Beginning. But as for you, are you too wise to join in and just play as well?"

"I am" Man told him. "But please be sure you make all the animals obey me if you will."

Now while they were talking, Pau Amma, the crab, decided he didn't want to take any orders from the Eldest Magician or from Man. So he scuttled off sideways and stepped into the sea to escape and play alone. Nobody saw the crab go except the man's little daughter from where she was sitting high up on his shoulders.

A little later, the Eldest Magician set off around the world to see how all the animals were getting on. He went North and found all the elephants digging with their tusks and stamping the nice new clean earth.

"Is this right?" asked the elephants.

"That is quite right," said the Eldest Magician. Then he went East and found all the cows. They were feeding in the fields, licking their tongues round bunches of grass. That was quite right too.

The Eldest Magician went West and found all the beavers making a beaver dam out of logs which they were pushing across the mouths of broad rivers. He was very pleased, it was just what he wanted.

In the South he found all the turtles scratching with their flippers in the sand. So he told them he was pleased with them as well.

By and by, the Eldest Magician met Man on the banks of the Perak River and asked him, "Son of Adam, are all the animals obedient to you?"

"Yes," said the man.

"And is all the earth obedient to you too?"

"Yes," replied the man again.

"What about the sea? Is that obedient to you as well?"

"No," said the man. "Once every day and every night, the sea runs up the Perak River and drives the sweet water back into the forests.

My house gets soaking wet. And once every day and night the sea runs down the river and pulls all the river water out with it, leaving nothing but mud. Then my canoe falls over on its side. Is that how you told the sea to behave?"

"No it is not," said the Eldest Magician.

"Look!" said the man, pointing. As he spoke the great sea rushed up the mouth of the Perak River, driving it backwards. It flowed into the forests for miles around and flooded the man's house.

"This is wrong," said the Eldest Magician, shaking his head. "Launch your canoe and we will find out who is playing with the sea."

So the magician, the man and his little daughter all stepped into the canoe and they pushed off down the Perak river. Then the sea started to run back down the river as well and the canoe was sucked out of the river mouth, far, far out to sea.

Then the moon rose big and full over the water. The Eldest Magician spoke to the hunchbacked old man who sits in the moon. "Hey there, old man. Is it you who is playing around with the sea?"

"No!" replied the old man. "I am busy spinning a fishing line, and when it's finished I hope I will catch the world with it. So I am far too busy to go playing around with the sea."

Now there is also a rat living on the moon who is always biting the fisherman's line in two before he can get it finished.

"Ho there, Rat of the Moon,"cried the Eldest Magician. "Is it you who is playing around with the sea?"

"I am too busy biting through the fisherman's line," replied the rat. "It isn't me who is playing around with the sea."

Then the man's daughter put out one little arm and said, "O Eldest Magician, while you were talking to my father at the Very Beginning and I was sitting on his shoulders, I saw one naughty animal crawling away into the sea. That was before you could teach him how to play."

"What was this animal like?" asked the Eldest Magician.

"He was round, and he was flat, and his eyes stuck out on stalks. He walked sideways too. Oh, and his back was covered with a shell."

"That sounds like Pau Amma to me. I was wondering where that wicked crab had got to.

Give me the paddle," he told the man, "and we will go and find him."

But they did not need to paddle hard for the sea flowed steadily. Soon it carried their canoe to the place called Pusat Tasek, the Heart of the Sea.

There the Eldest Magician slid his arm right down into the deep warm water until he touched the broad back of Pau Amma, the crab. When the Magician touched him, Pau Amma settled down, and all the sea rose up just like it does when you put your hand in a basin of water.

"Ah," said the Eldest Magician, "now I know who has been playing with the sea. Pau Amma, what do you think you're playing at?"

From deep down below, Pau Amma answered him. "Once a day and once a night I go out to look for my food. And once a day and once a night I come back again. Now go away and leave me alone."

"Listen to me, Pau Amma," said the Eldest Magician. "When you go out from your cave, the waters of the sea pour down and fill up the Heart of the Sea where you were sitting. Then all the beaches on all the islands are left bare. The little fish die and the elephants legs get muddy. Then when you go back and sit in the Heart of the Sea again, all the water in the sea rises again. Then half the little islands are drowned, the Man's house is flooded, and the crocodiles' mouths are filled with water."

Pau Amma just laughed. "I didn't know I was so important. From now on I think I'll go out seven times a day so the sea will never be still."

"Pau Amma, I cannot make you behave the way I want," said the Eldest Magician. "And that's because you ran off in the Very Beginning. But if you're not scared of me, come up and let's talk about it."

“I’m not afraid,” said Pau Amma, floating up to the top of the sea where the moonlight shone on him brightly. Nobody in the world was as big as Pau Amma – for he was the king of all the crabs. His great shell stretched for hundreds of miles, and he was taller than a huge mountain. As Pau Amma rose to the top of the sea, he pushed through the branches of the Wonderful Tree and tore off one of the great, magic nuts which make people young. And the little girl saw it bobbing beside the canoe. She pulled it in and started to pick out the nut’s soft centre with a pair of little golden scissors.

“If you are so important,” the Magician said to Pau Amma, “why don’t you do some magic for me?” Pau Amma rolled his eyes and waved his legs but he could only stir up the sea.

“See! You are not so important after all,” laughed the Magician. “Now let ME try.”

Then, using just the little finger of his left hand, he did some magic. Suddenly Pau Amma's hard blue-green-black shell fell off him. Pau Amma was left all soft. "I bet you don't feel so important now," said the Magician. "Shall I get the Man here to cut your soft back with his knife. Or should I call for the elephants and get them to pierce it with their tusks? Then again, perhaps the crocodile would like a tasty snack."

"I'm very sorry," Pau Amma pleaded. "Give me back my shell and I promise I will only go out once a day and once a night to get my food."

"No, I will not give you back your shell," was the reply. "If I do, you will grow bigger and stronger and forget your promise to stop playing around with the sea."

Pau Amma waved his legs and cried.

"I cannot make you behave properly," the Magician continued, "because you got away from me in the Very Beginning. But if you like, I can make every part of the sea just as safe as the Heart of the Sea for you and your children."

"Before I make up my mind," said Pau Amma, "let's see what the Man will do for me. If he hadn't stopped to talk to you I would not have got fed up waiting and run away. So what will he do to make up for it?"

"If you like," said Man, "I will do some magic so that both the sea and the land will be home for you and your children. Then there will be lots of places for you to hide."

"That sounds good too," replied the crab,

"but before I make up my mind let me hear from the little girl. If she hadn't seen me I wouldn't be in this fix."

The little girl said, "This is a good nut I'm eating. If you like I will do some magic and give you this very strong sharp pair of scissors. Then you and your children could use them to eat coconuts like this all day long when you come out onto the land."

Pau Amma thought hard about all this. "Because I am so soft, even if I took all of these gifts they would not help me. Give me back my shell, Eldest Magician, and I promise I will behave as you want me to."

"Well, you shall have your shell back,Pau Amma," said the Eldest Magician, "but only for eleven months of the year. In the twelfth month it will grow soft again to remind you and your children of my powerful magic."

Pau Amma thought a little while. "I have made up my mind," he said. "I will take all the gifts."

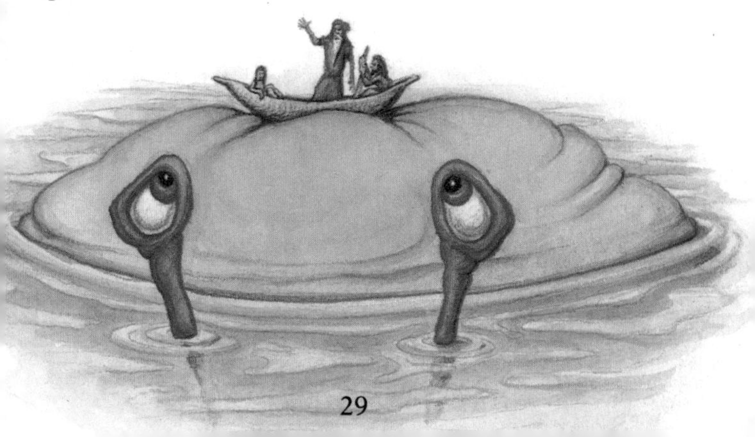

So the Eldest Magician cast a spell with his right hand and suddenly Pau Amma grew smaller and smaller until at last there was only a little green crab swimming in the water crying, "Give me the scissors," in a tiny voice. The little girl picked him up in the palm of her hand and gave him the scissors. The Magician blessed the little crab and he scuttled off happily into the water.

The Eldest Magician was feeling pleased with himself now that he had solved the problem of what to do with Pau Amma. But the man was fed up. "Now we have to go all the way back to Perak - and that's a long way to paddle. If we had waited till Pau Amma had left the Heart of the Sea, the water would have carried us home by itself."

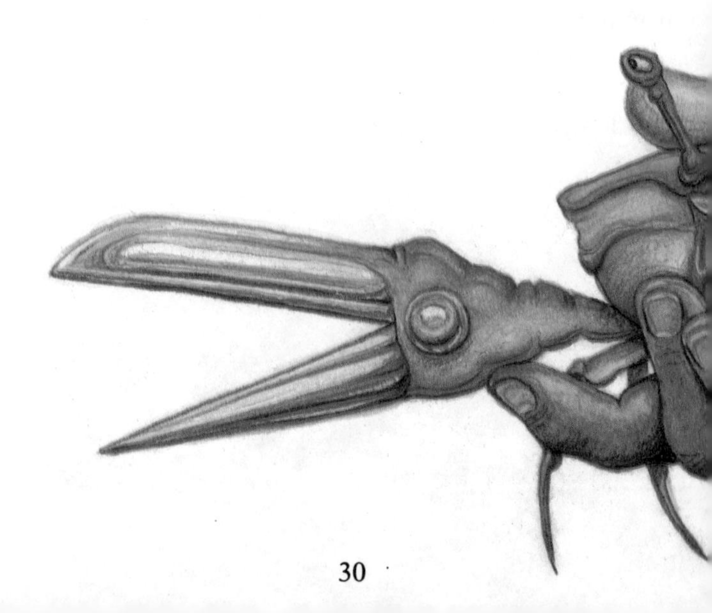

"You are lazy," scolded the Eldest Magician. "So your children shall be lazy too. They shall be the laziest creatures in the world." He held up his fingers to the moon and said,

"O Fisherman, look at this man. He is too lazy even to row home. Pull his canoe home with your line."

"No," said the Man, "if I am to be lazy for the rest of my life, let the sea work for me twice a day for ever. That will save me the trouble of paddling."

The Eldest Magician laughed and said, "Let it be so." So the Rat in the Moon stopped biting the line, and the Fisherman let it down until it touched the sea. Then he pulled the whole sea along until the canoe whirled into the mouth of the Perak River again. The Magician instructed the Fisherman to pull the sea twice a day from that day on, and that is how we have tides.

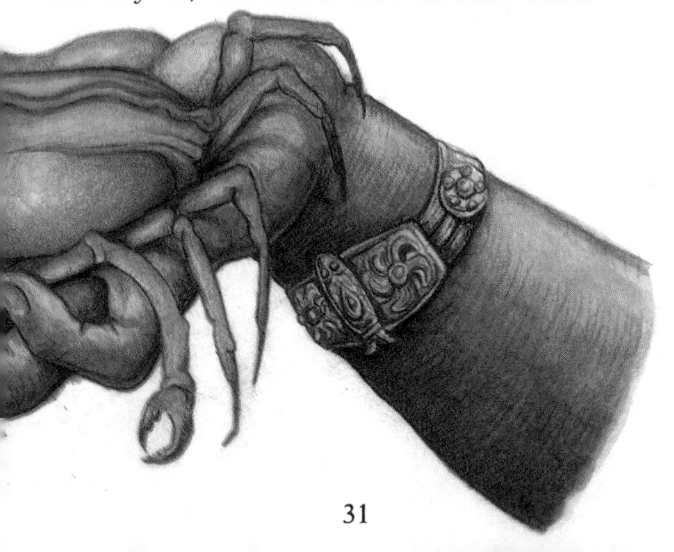

The Magician, the man and his daughter all carried on up the Perak River, and when they reached home they went to bed.

And Pau Amma?

Well, when you go to the beach you can see how all the crabs make little safe hiding places for themselves under the stones and bunches of seaweed. You can watch them waving their little scissors, and in some parts of the world, you can see they really do live on dry land and run up palm trees and eat coconuts. But once a year all the crabs shake off their hard shells and show their soft backs to remind them of what the Eldest Magician could do if he wanted. And all of this has come about because old Pau Amma was so stupidly rude a very long time ago.

Carnival is an imprint of
HarperCollins Publishers Ltd
77-85 Fulham Palace Road,
Hammersmith, London W6 8JB

First published by Carnival in 1991

ISBN 0 00 192639 X

Printed in Great Britain by
BPCC Hazell Books, Paulton and Aylesbury